This is Lop,
Bod's big sister.

This is Bod, Lop's
little brother.

5

Bod, Lop and the other children split up into pairs and rushed off with the teacher's list. They all wanted to win prizes!

Bod and Lop decided to start in the Animal Room. They didn't know where it was, so Lop asked a guard.

W A L K E R   B O O K S
AND SUBSIDIARIES
LONDON · BOSTON · SYDNEY

Under this flap, and the one on page 23, you'll find lots of extra things to spot in the big pictures.

When you have finished reading the story, open out the flaps and start searching!

This is the story of Bod and Lop and a chase to catch a thief.

They were on a school trip to the Space Museum on Planet Zog. Their teacher gave each child a list of ten things to spot. The winners would get prizes.

But Bod and Lop spotted something else instead! They got into some very tricky situations and had to solve a lot of puzzles along the way.

Can you help Bod and Lop?

- **Read the story and solve the puzzles.**

- **Check your answers at the back when you reach the end, or if you get really stuck.**

The guard told them to go up the yellow staircases, down the green staircases and through the open door.

Can you help them find the way to the Animal Room?

Bod and Lop found the Animal Room and went in. "Look at that!" shouted Bod, running over to a Cosmos dog.

They spent ages in the room, but then Lop noticed the time. "We'd better look at the rest of the museum," she said.

This is how the room looked as they were leaving.

As they were leaving, Lop remembered the list, so they turned back. "Something's been stolen!" gasped Bod.

 Look at the two pictures below.

What did Bod notice was missing?

Can you see six other things that have moved or disappeared?

This is how it looked when they turned back.

Bod and Lop told the guard about the stolen frog. "Let's see if we can find the thief with the spy cameras," she said.

The children studied the screens carefully as the guard checked every room in the museum. "There's the thief!" yelled Lop.

"That's the Sports Room," said the guard and off they zoomed.

The room was so crowded that it was hard to see anything at all! "Look out for the bright yellow gloves," cried the guard.

Can you spot the thief?

At last they saw the thief. "Can you go and get help while I keep an eye on him?" whispered the guard.

"You'll find more guards in the café. My name is Tag. Tell them I sent you."

Bod and Lop raced to the café as fast as they could.

Can you help them spot the guards? There are six, all drinking their favourite rainbow shakes and wearing green uniforms.

13

Bod and Lop told the guards about the thief, and they all ran over to the spy camera screens to see where he was now.

Lop spotted him going into the Robot Room, so they rushed there next. Tag was waiting. "He can't escape!" she said.

But the moment they entered the Robot Room, the thief fired his Scramble Zapper gun and filled it with green smoke.

When the smoke cleared, the thief had disappeared. The Scramble Zapper gun had made six robots do naughty things.

Can you spot the six naughty robots?

The Zapper gun had also messed up the spy cameras.
"Let's split up and search the museum," said Tag.

Bod and Lop were sent to tell Mr Sprog, the museum owner, about the thief. They found him in the Clothes Room.

Mr Sprog was very flustered. The thief had mixed up the clothes on four of the models with his Scramble Zapper gun.

Can you help Bod, Lop and Mr Sprog sort out the four outfits and put them back on the models? Match the colours to the stands.

Bod looked out of the window and saw the thief in the museum gardens. "Quick! Let's follow him!" yelled Mr Sprog.

But when they got outside the thief had gone. "He must be heading for the spaceship park," said Mr Sprog.

Can you help them find their way to the spaceship park? Don't go on paths blocked by spiky orange balls.

Tag and some of the other guards arrived at the spaceship park. "Where's the thief?" asked Tag.

Then Bod saw him. He was firing his Scramble Zapper gun at the other spaceships so they wouldn't work.

The only spaceship the thief didn't break was his own.

Can you help the guards find the thief's spaceship before he escapes in it?

The guards caught the thief just in time. "Thank you both for all your help," Mr Sprog said to the two children.

Then Lop remembered the teacher's list. "We'll never win prizes now!" she sighed. "I'll give you prizes," said Mr Sprog.

We have three yellow eyes,
We're furry and blue,
With pink curly tails
And pink noses too.
What are we?

Mr Sprog took Bod and Lop to the museum shop. "Your prizes are in here," he said. "Can you solve this riddle to see what they are?"

Can you help Bod and Lop solve the riddle and find the two prizes?

Under this flap, and the one on page 4, you'll find lots of extra things to spot in the big pictures.

When you have finished reading the story, open out the flaps and start searching!

The Answers

- The answers to the story puzzles are shown with single black lines.

- The answers to the fun flap puzzles are shown with double black lines.

Pages 4 and 5

Pages 6 and 7

Pages 8 and 9

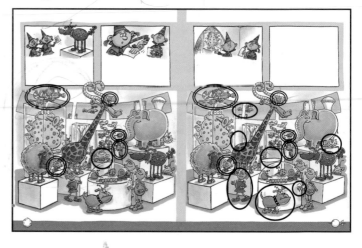

Pages 10 and 11

Pages 12 and 13

Pages 14 and 15

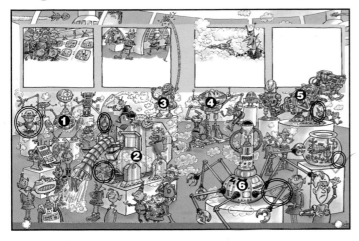

Pages 16 and 17

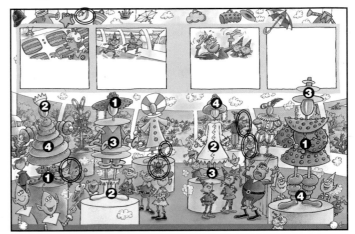

Pages 18 and 19

Pages 20 and 21

Pages 22 and 23